SECRET SPY SOCIETY

the CASE of the CURIOUS SCOUTS

Veronica Mang

VIKING

VIKING
An imprint of Penguin Random House LLC, New York

First published in the United States of America by Viking,
an imprint of Penguin Random House LLC, 2022

Visit us online at penguinrandomhouse.com.

Library of Congress Cataloging-in-Publication Data is available.

Printed in the United States of America

ISBN 9780593204382

10 9 8 7 6 5 4 3 2 1

LSCC

Design by Kate Renner

Text set in New Baskerville ITC Infant

The art for this book was made using graphite and gouache, and then colored digitally.

To Serena,
my first friend and closest confidante

Chapter ONE

In a gloomy town filled with rain and snow, all was quiet and still. Dusk stretched slowly over the streets, while snow fell like powdered sugar over a donut. If you were a stranger passing through, you might assume that nothing out of the ordinary ever happened here. But if you looked closely—very closely—you might notice a tall, skinny house on a nondescript street. That house belonged to the Secret Spy Society. The curtains were drawn, but a warm light glowed inside, where three girls were about to stumble upon a new adventure.

The Secret Spy Society was made up of the Lady Spies, notorious and accomplished secret agents. But there was also a special division called the Petite Private Eyes, which was made up of little girls named Peggy, Rita, and Dot. They were only spies in training but each had her own unique skills and accomplishments.

Perhaps it was unusual for children their age to be studying espionage, but then again, Peggy, Rita, and Dot were not like most others. Tonight, the girls had visited the Lady Spies in the hopes of finding some adventure, but instead found themselves stuck with . . . homework. Spies must know the ins and outs of the world and that begins with social studies, reading, and math . . . or at least that's what the Lady Spies told the girls whenever they complained about their schoolwork.

Rita, who loved reading, thinking hard, and solving tricky problems, was staring intently at her paper and retracing her steps through a particularly puzzling bit of algebra.

Dot, who loved action and making things with her hands, found herself drifting from her social studies homework and instead folding airplanes out of her notes. Occasionally she flung one across the room and sprinted after it.

Peggy, who loved jokes, tricks, and sweet-talking, was *not* particularly excited about tedious equations and dreary literary classics. She had abandoned her homework entirely and was instead revisiting an earlier project.

All was silent . . .

PEGGY

until she raised two fingers to her lips and let out a glorious *fwoooooot!* that echoed around the room.

A steady *buh-dump, buh-dump* began to drift from somewhere deeper inside the house. It grew louder and louder until . . .

= mrrrow!

A flurry of dots and fluff soared into the room and landed on the middle of the table, scattering pens and papers.

It was Chiquita, Josephine Baker's pet cheetah! Dot and Rita nearly toppled out of their chairs. They tried to look stern but broke into a fit of giggles.

Chiquita looked very proud of herself. "Homework is important, but so are new tricks!" Peggy grinned.

The girls' laughs were interrupted by a sudden

Ding Dong!

at the front door.

Miss Khan appeared from the shadows of the house, silent as the falling snow outside. She was the girls' schoolteacher, and a few months ago they discovered that she was also part of the Secret Spy Society. They watched from the table as she crouched down and crept up to the door, looked through the peephole, and then sighed. She opened the door to reveal two women outside, looking very upset.

It was the Fashion Twins, Josephine Baker's long-time dress designers. They wore stylish clothes with bits of thread stuck to their stockings. Cece had big, beautiful curls, and Yuki kept a beret neatly perched upon her head. They both wore perfectly identical chic glasses, which is how they got their name.

"Oh no. What happened to them?" Rita whispered.

The girls often visited the Fashion Twins' store to pick up dresses for Josephine, and the Fashion Twins were always cheerful and silly. But today was different: tears streaked their cheeks and their glasses were fogged from crying.

"Something horrible has happened!" they cried.

Peggy, Rita, and Dot watched wide-eyed as Miss Khan led the Fashion Twins to the living room, where some of the other spies were relaxing.

She handed them a box of tissues. "Please—tell me what's wrong," she said kindly.

"Well," explained Yuki, "we were out for dinner—"

"We came back to the shop—" Cece continued.

"And the dresses were scattered all over the place—" Yuki added.

"And there were footprints—" They gulped.

"And mud—"

"Someone stole one of our dresses!" the women cried in unison. Upon sharing this news, they burst into tears.

Miss Khan and the other spies gathered around to listen intently.

"Those dresses are our life's work!" Cece cried, wiping the fog from her glasses.

Up until this point, Peggy, Rita, and Dot had sat quietly at their table trying very hard to look busy but, like any good spies, were unable to keep themselves from eavesdropping. Stolen dresses? Mysterious footprints? Peggy couldn't hold it in any longer. "We'll help!" she exclaimed.

Cecily Lefort

Mary Jane
Richards Denman

Sarah
Emma
Edmonds

Nancy Wake

Josephine Baker

Christine Granville

Sarah Aaronsohn

Yolande Beekman

Violette Szabo

Noor Inayat Khan

Odette Hallowes

15

The twins looked startled, as if to say, *Is that even allowed?*

Peggy batted her eyes. "Well, after all, you Lady Spies are *very* busy with your *other* projects, and our schedule is wide open!"

Dot and Rita sprung from the table. "Homework can wait!" they cheered, dashing for their coats.

Cece was baffled. "Now?" she said. "It's getting dark and it's snowing!"

Rita nodded. "Evidence only lasts for so long, and it's important that we start our investigation immediately."

The Fashion Twins looked to Miss Khan, who shrugged. "It's true," she said, pausing to think. "Take Chiquita! She'll keep you safe, and she's excellent at tracking!"

The girls walked over to shake the Fashion Twins' hands.

"Petite Private Eyes, at your service!"

One by one, Peggy, Rita,
Dot, and Chiquita piled into
the Fashion Twins' car and headed to the
shop. When they arrived, it was obvious why Cece
and Yuki were upset. All around them, spools
of thread were littered on the floor and odds
and ends of fabric were scattered around the
room.

Yuki held up a dress. "*This* one is torn!"

Cece laid out another. "*This* one is covered in
muddy footprints!"

Yuki laid out one more. "And *this* one is all
smeared with . . ."

Peggy, Rita, and Dot gathered around. "What *is* that?" Rita asked with disgust.

Dot, ever the adventurer, stepped forward. She sniffed, scooped a glob onto her finger, sniffed again. And then . . .

Peggy and Rita shrieked, "*Ewww!*"

Dot licked the pink-something off of her finger. Then she giggled. "It's jelly!"

"Jelly?" echoed the Fashion Twins.

The girls were mystified. How odd, and how . . . *sticky.*

"We need more clues," said Rita.

They looked under
the sewing machine.

They looked inside
the thread drawer.
They looked inside
the storage closet.

They even looked under a big taffeta gown.

Dot sighed, slouching against the windowsill.

"This feels pointless. Clearly, whoever did this was a real pro." She rubbed her face in exhaustion.

Peggy and Rita giggled. "Dot, your face is covered in . . . glitter!"

Dot looked at her hands, which were twinkling. "Ah-ha!" The windowsill in front of her was covered in

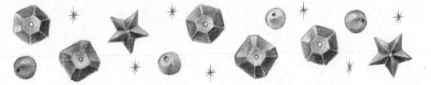

a layer of glittering rhinestones and twinkling sequins. She cracked the window open and began to climb out. "Let's go!"

The Fashion Twins looked baffled.

"Is this safe?" Yuki and Cece asked in perfect synchronization.

"Don't worry," said Dot, one foot out of the window. "We have Chiquita! And besides, we're professionals!"

Outside, snow fell around them as glitter flashed under the streetlights.

"Quick!" huffed Dot. "We need to pick up the pace—the snow is covering the trail!"

Chiquita understood. She dashed ahead playfully.

"Not too fast!" giggled Rita. "We're not cheetahs!"

The twinkling trail led them through town, and they followed through darkness and snow until they reached the back of a shadowy house. All sorts of strange noises were coming from inside—hooting, hollering, laughing, yelling.

"What is this place?" asked Peggy with wide eyes.

Dot looked determined. "Only one way to find out." She approached a low basement window and peered inside.

"Are those . . . scouts?" Children were bouncing off of furniture, and a few very frustrated-looking children were trying to work, occasionally shushing.

"This can't be the right place," whispered Rita. "Why would these scouts be stealing Yuki and Cece's beautiful dresses?"

Beats me," whispered Dot. "We must have made a mistake. It happens to the best of spies." But then she gasped. "Is that . . . *jelly?*"

In the middle of the room, one scout was sitting, happily eating a big, drippy, sticky, messy . . . *jelly donut.* "Just like the jelly on the dress!" hissed Peggy.

The girls moved away from the window.

"This doesn't make sense," said Dot.

"We need more intel," said Rita, shaking her head. "Wait a second. This sounds like the perfect time for a stakeout!"

"Sure," said Peggy. "But I'm freezing. Let's go home!" Chiquita's nose was dripping, and her fur was powdered with snow. They hurried home and slept deeply, with dreams of glitter and donuts and raucous children.

–*–*–*–

The following day, the girls met at their own club-house, which happened to be in Rita's attic. Although they liked to spend time at the Secret Spy Society, their clubhouse was perfect for board games and sleepovers and preparing for last-minute operations.

"A stakeout," said Peggy with a sly grin. The girls were packing Rita's handy bag. "What do we need?" She pulled out a suitcase from under the bed. It was stuffed to the brim with old accessories from Rita's mother, and a strange assortment of Halloween costumes.

"Nothing   much," said Rita. "Binoculars, sunglasses—"

"A steak?" said Dot with a giggle.

"Maybe, with your appetite!" Rita shot back with a giggle. Dot was a notorious snacker and was currently munching on a prehistoric sandwich she had unearthed from Rita's bag.

Peggy tossed sunglasses at the other girls. "Let's roll."

Chapter TWO

As soon as they were finished with school the next day, the girls retraced their steps from the night before and were surprised to find a lavish house waiting for them in the daylight. A fence stood guard in front of a manicured lawn, and immaculately trimmed shrubbery traced the sidewalk. The girls kept their distance and lingered at a café down the block. ("Perfect for stakeout snacks!" Dot said.) Rita dug through her bag, which was loaded with odds and ends that most children would never think of: tape measures, markers that could write in invisible ink, even a windup toy. ("For creating diversions!" Rita always said.) She pulled out binoculars and peered through as they assumed position: hats pulled down, scarves hiked up, snacks at the ready, and a notebook poised for note-taking in Peggy's lap.

"Something's happening!" hissed Rita.

"What do you see?" Peggy elbowed Rita and grabbed for the binoculars.

"*Shhh!* This is a *stakeout!*" Rita muttered, elbowing back. "There's kids outside. Mowing the lawn. Another one is trimming the bushes. And a different scout is cleaning the windows." Peggy took notes at a ferocious speed.

"Wait . . . These are the kids from last night!" said Rita. Dot almost choked on her pizza. "I see someone inside. A lady. She's instructing them from the window. Who is she?"

They peeked through the binoculars one by one.

"Why are they doing chores?" mumbled Dot through cheesy bites.

At that moment, the lady in the house looked up and seemed to stare right back at them.

"*Eeeeek!*" shrieked Dot. "Time to go!" They brushed the crumbs off of their jackets and hurried around the corner, out of sight.

The girls retreated to the Secret Spy Society, feeling very defeated. They were greeted by the Lady Spies, who were gathered around the living room sipping hot coffees and reading books. The girls collapsed on the sofa in a huff.

"Hello, girls!" Miss Khan waved cheerfully. "Fancy a snack?"

Peggy took a cookie and munched glumly as she explained the situation. "We're no closer to figuring out what happened to the missing dress!"

Rita sighed. "We're at a dead end."

Odette Hallowes leaned forward. "Don't fret, girls. It happens to the best of us!"

Violette Szabo nodded. "Sometimes you just need a new angle."

Miss Khan sat up a bit straighter. "*Ah-ha!*" she exclaimed, hopping from her seat and extending a hand to pull the girls out of their slump. "I know just the person to help!"

She led them up the winding staircase into a part of the house they had never been to before. A door was tucked neatly at the end of the hall. Miss Khan knocked, and it opened.

Sitting in a chair was an elegant woman. She had been hunched over a book, deep in thought, but she glanced up as the girls entered. She gave them a big smile, and a twinkle danced in her eyes.

"Dindy!" cheered Peggy, Rita, and Dot.

It was Virginia Hall, or "Dindy," as her fellow Lady Spies called her. She always had a joke to tell and a trick up her sleeve. Virginia made everything a grand adventure and seemed to be filled with endless energy. She was usually on a covert mission to some top-secret location. But today . . .

"You're back!" the girls cheered. Virginia rose from her desk as the girls dashed forward to surround her in a bundle of hugs.

"Hello, girls! What sort of mischief are you up to now?" she said with a sly grin.

"We're totally stuck on our latest case," explained Dot.

Peggy nodded vigorously. "Something fishy is going on inside that house."

Virginia thought for a moment. "It sounds like someone is *hiding* something." She raised an eyebrow, pivoted on her heel, and turned to a bookcase behind her. With a mischievous grin, she pulled a nondescript book from the bottom of the shelf. At first nothing

happened, but suddenly there was a loud *guh-bonk!* and the bookcase swung away from the wall to reveal a hid-den door!

"One of the most useful skills for a spy is the ability to go undercover!" Virginia stood up and pulled a few hangers from the hidden closet. "Who wants to go first?"

They tried fancy costumes.
Cool costumes.
Ill-fitting costumes.

And costumes that were just *all* wrong.

Finally, at the back of the closet, they found them. "My old sporting uniforms!" Virginia cheered in delight. "I knew they would be useful someday!"

The girls tried them on and then stepped out for their grand reveal.

"We look just like those scouts!" Peggy squealed, and did a little dance to show off her new uniform, while Rita did a celebratory twirl and Dot tumbled into a cartwheel.

"Costumes are great, but there are even more techniques for going undercover. For example"—Virginia sat up straight, pursed her lips, and began to talk in a very high, scrunched-up voice—"like this! You can draw attention to something very specific, like a unique speaking style or a strange laugh, which can distract from your true identity." The girls gave it a try. Rita sounded gruff, Dot sounded sleepy, and Peggy worked her voice into a rich, pleasant drawl that made her sound like she was from somewhere very far away.

Virginia cheered. "Exactly! You can also put something in your shoe to change the way you walk." She opened a drawer and pulled out a few carefully chiseled pieces of wood, which they slipped into their shoes. Rita's walk became careful and prim and proper, Peggy adopted a different gait that shuffled like a dance, and Dot took to walking like a pirate.

"Very good!" Virginia laughed.

Virginia perched herself on a poufy ottoman. "You know, sometimes things seem like obstacles when they are actually a special strength."

"What do you mean?" asked Peggy.

"Well, just like my leg!" She extended her left leg, which was wooden from the knee down. It gave her a distinct walk but never seemed to slow her down. Virginia gave it a pat and laughed. "I call him Cuthbert!" The girls giggled, too.

"When I was injured, I thought my days of adventure were over. But like any good spy, I knew I couldn't give in that easily! And you know what? My leg helped me go undercover time and time again. I could even slip secret notes into my metal ankle!" She winked. "But don't tell anyone!" Virginia smiled, but the girls knew that she had a lot to teach them, and not just about espionage.

A few days later, the girls geared up for their undercover expedition. All week they had rehearsed their stories, practiced their walks, and perfected their voices. Finally, the night had come. They put on Virginia's old uniforms and headed back to the mysterious house.

The girls approached the cellar door uneasily. "Just one last thing to add to your disguise," said Rita. She lifted Peggy's hat up and fluffed up her hair, then smeared a bit of mud on Dot's cheek.

She raised her fist to knock, but before her hand even touched the door, it opened a crack. A set of eyes peered out at them.

"What?" asked the figure behind the door.

The girls glanced at one another, unnerved. Peggy took a quick breath in and out. Only Dot and Rita could tell that she was nervous.

"We're new scouts from a different troop. Transfers!" She gave a big smile.

The mysterious figure peeked out more, and the girls could make out a scrunched-up, angry-looking face. It was a scout: messy hair flopped over his forehead, eyes darkened by a stiff scout hat.

"Transfers?" He grunted. "Scout Leader didn't mention anything about *transfers.*"

Peggy shrugged. "Must've forgotten!"

The scout looked them up and down, scrunched his face even more, and then slammed the door shut. Peggy gave Rita and Dot a look that said, *Mission abort!*

They were ready to return home and nurse their bruised egos over a cup of cocoa when suddenly they heard the lock slide. "I'm Finch. Come inside," said the scout as he swung the door open. "We could use the help, anyway." He rolled his eyes rudely and spun around on his heels with a huff.

In the basement, scouts were scattered all around, along with boxes of supplies and messy, teetering stacks of paper.

As they entered, the room fell silent. Scouts froze in the middle of their activities and shot angry stares in the girls' direction.

"Who are *they*?" shouted a kid in the back.

Finch shrugged. "Transfers," he muttered, as if he wasn't quite sure what to do with Peggy, Rita, and Dot.

The scouts got up from their perches and formed a circle around the girls. Peggy crossed her arms and adopted a tough expression on her

face. Rita and Dot followed her lead, giving curt nods to the scouts.

Finch grunted. "That's Twig." He pointed one by one to the kids in the circle. "And that's Crumb, Smudge, Cat, Pinky, Darling, Doc, Toots, Pippy, and Cash." Despite their scowls, they seemed bashful upon being introduced. Some even blushed.

"And who are *you*?" asked Finch, turning to the girls.

"Uhhhh . . . I'm Peggy."

"Dot."

"And I'm Rita."

Finch was silent for a moment. "Those names are ridiculous," he grumbled.

The other scouts mumbled in agreement.

"Um, Finch . . . What exactly do we do now?" asked Peggy as they shuffled along next to him.

Finch sighed. "Well, look around!" He flung his hand up in the air and his face flushed red. "*Someone* has to do all these scout duties!" The girls looked at the teetering stacks of paper and boxes and mops and messes but weren't sure what *that* had to do with scouting.

"What do you *mean*, exactly?" asked Dot.

Finch flopped down on a worn-out chair behind a worn-out desk and exhaled slowly, his face gradually returning to a normal color. He reached under the desk and lifted a tall stack of papers. They landed on the desk with a *thud*.

"Mathematics Badge."

The girls exchanged glances. Rita pulled a sheet from the top of the stack. "Is this . . . ?"

"Taxes," said Finch.

"That sounds—"

"Horrible, I know." He yanked the paper from Rita's hand and gently smoothed it out on the desk. "Scout Leader says if we get enough badges, we can go on a camping trip! And besides, this is what *all* scouts do. See?" He held up a very official-looking paper with a row of checked boxes labeled MATHEMATICS BADGE.

Rita read along: "'In order to earn the prestigious Mathematics Badge, you must first file Scout Leader's taxes.'"

Finch puffed out his chest. "This is our assignment, and I'm going to be the best scout I can be!" But then he seemed to deflate, sinking deeper into the chair. "This sure is boring, though."

Now that they were up close, the girls realized that Finch wasn't mean; he was tired. They looked at the other scouts working feverishly. Darling had even fallen asleep over her stack of electrical bills. They were the same age as the girls, yet they looked far older.

"Can you tell us about some of your other badges?" asked Peggy, perching on the edge of Finch's desk. "We're a little behind on our own and it would be a big help."

Finch pulled himself up from the crumbly chair. "Well, this one"—he pointed to a badge with what appeared to be a toothbrush on it—

"was my Cleanliness Badge, for scrubbing Scout Leader's floors. And this one"—he pointed to a badge with an embroidered carrot—"is a Nutrition Badge, for making Scout Leader one hundred peanut butter sandwiches! And this one"—he pointed to a badge with a cat and dog on it—"is a Veterinary Badge, for grooming Scout Leader's poodle."

"Poodle?" asked Peggy, nearly breaking character. Finch nodded solemnly and gestured to Pinky, who was in the corner wrangling a small but aggressive dog into a pair of booties. Peggy contained a laugh and instead

nodded. "Thanks, Finch—
that will give us a big head
start! We'll go . . . find
something to work on."

"I'm sure they need help upstairs."
Finch returned to his stack of papers.

"Yikes," whispered Peggy as they walked away. "One
hundred peanut butter sandwiches? *Taxes?* What kind
of scout troop is this?"

They headed up a rickety staircase that led to the
kitchen, where Doc was elbows-deep in dirty sink water.

"Hey, you!" she called as she scrubbed intensely
at a dirty bowl. "It's two o'clock. Scout Leader needs
her peanut butter sandwich. Take that up to her." Doc
nodded toward a sandwich, crusts perfectly removed,
plated neatly with some grapes, which she had miracu-
lously managed to peel. "Just how she likes it!"

"You do this . . . every day?" asked Peggy, examining
a grape. Doc scoffed and pointed to the carrot badge
on her vest. "Nutrition Badge. Obviously."

Peggy nodded, as if that made sense. "We'll take
this to her," she said.

The girls continued to the living
room, observing as the scouts did
all sort of things: scrubbed the

floors, touched up paint on the wall, polished spoons, and carefully ironed shirts. "I know that scouts are supposed to be helpful but isn't this a little extreme?" whispered Dot. Then she froze, gently nudging the others. "Look at that!"

Down the hall was a tall wooden door. A tidy sign read NO SCOUTS ALLOWED, but to Peggy, Rita, and Dot, it might as well have said, *Come on in!* They immediately made a beeline down the hall.

Rita fished a screwdriver from her bag and discretely passed it to Dot while Peggy kept watch. Only a few moments passed before there was a soft *click* and the door popped open.

They hurried inside, and the door shut behind them with a heavy

=THUD.=

The girls found themselves plunged into complete darkness.

"Where's the light?!" hissed Peggy, grabbing the air in front of her but only finding one of Dot's pigtails.

"Hold on!" whispered Rita as she dug in her bag. A grape rolled from the plate and

SCOUT NOTES

went *squelch!* under her foot.

Finally, she found a flashlight for each of them. Books lined the walls, and a wooden desk sat heavily in the middle of the room. "This must be her office!" hissed Rita. They moved slowly, careful not to step on the bits of trash that littered the floor.

"Looks like she's helpless without the scouts," said Peggy, pinching her nose. The whole room smelled like old socks, and stacks of dirty plates were set precariously around the room.

DONUTS

Pssssssst!

hissed Dot. "Look at this!"
Perched conspicuously on
the desk was none other
than a half-eaten box
of jelly donuts. "Just like
the jelly from the dress!"

"And check this out!" whispered Peggy. The ground was
dusted in twinkling sequins, and
nearly hidden in the rubble was a distinct

tag with a pair of cat-eyed glasses: the Fashion Twins!

Rita, who had been peeking through drawers, suddenly gasped. She gently pulled out a book: "'Scout Leader Handbook,'" she read aloud. They began to flip through pages about the importance of truth and kindness. Finally, the book fell open to a well-worn page.

NUTRITION BADGE: Scouts will learn the fundamentals of cooking and healthy eating, laying the groundwork for self-reliance and self-care.

~~MAKE ME A SNACK!~~

GARDENING BADGE: Scouts will learn the basics of keeping a garden, including planting seedlings with supervision, cooking with fresh food, and time spent volunteering at a community garden.

TRIM THE BUSHES

LEATHERWORKING BADGE: Scouts will have a new appreciation for craftsmanship as we learn the fundamentals of leatherworking. Suggested projects include: braiding basics, overview of tools, and a trip to a tannery or other local leather-working business.

POLISH MY SHOES!!

VETERINARY BADGE: Instill an early love of animals through the study of pets and other creatures. Activities include: discuss difference between reptiles, mammals, birds, and fish. Learn fundamentals of pet care. Visit to a local animal clinic or shelter highly recommended.

(handwritten) GROOM MY DOG!!

HOME IMPROVEMENT BADGE: Empower your scouts as they learn repair basics. Suggested activities: fundamentals of power tools, building a birdhouse, painting a room.

(handwritten) UNCLOG THE TOILET

SEWING & TEXTILE BADGE: With this badge, scouts will learn the fundamentals of sewing and design. Suggested subjects include: Braiding, knotting, and embroidery. Threading a needle. Visit to local fashion designer highly recommend

(handwritten) IRON MY SHIRT!!

The girls were speechless. They exchanged looks that said: *Are you thinking what I'm thinking?*

The girls hurried from the room, book in hand, and found Finch still at the desk and buried in tax papers.

"Finch!" shouted Peggy. "We need to talk to you." He shooed them away. "Can't you see I'm busy? I'm trying to earn us a camping trip."

"Scout Leader is lying to you," said Rita. "Look at this!"

"Yeah, sure," said Finch, eyes still glued to his work.

Dot groaned and dropped the book in front of him. "Finch, these are the tasks you *should* be doing! Not her crummy taxes!"

"What are you talking about?" asked Finch. He rose from his rickety chair.

"See for yourself!" said Peggy, gesturing to the book. Finch picked it up.

"'Insect Badge,'" he read aloud as the other scouts drifted over and formed a circle around them. "'Awarded to scouts after they successfully complete their local entomology worksheet. Overnight camping trip recommended.'"

"Entomology worksheet?" said Darling.

"We've never been on a *camping* trip!" shouted Twig.

Finch's face flushed a hot red. "And get this! She has a note in here that says, 'Have scouts remove wasp nest from porch.' Remember when we did that?" He threw his hands up in frustration. "That was a horrible day!"

The scouts shouted in protest.

"And look at this!" he continued. "For Cleanliness Badge, she wrote, 'Scouts will clean dishes and scrub

the floor.'" Finch froze with big eyes, rubber gloves still covered in soap.

Finch flipped the page and a few photographs suddenly fell from the book. They drifted slowly to the ground and the room fell into an icy silence. Doc stepped forward and the color drained from her face.

"It's Scout Leader. She's . . ."

The scouts erupted into roars and wails.

"She went camping *without* us?" roared Pinky.

"After all we've done?" sobbed Toots through angry tears.

The scouts were beginning to piece together the strange truth when Rita noticed one more piece of paper on the ground. "What is this?!" she asked. The children crouched down to get a closer look.

Rita read aloud: "'Please join us for a gala evening as we celebrate the prestigious Scout Leader of the Year Award, given each year to the scout leader with the most badges earned. This year's recipient: Scout Leader Smith.'" The girls' stomachs knotted with dread. "She must have stolen the dress to attend the gala!" cried Peggy.

"And look at the time!" said Dot. "She's probably on her way there now!"

Finch looked horrified. Rita, however, was already one step ahead. "Meet us there at seven p.m." The girls pivoted and were on their way out when Finch called to them.

"You aren't scouts, are you?" he asked.

"We're the Petite Private Eyes," said Dot with a grin. "And right now, we've got a job to do."

Chapter THREE

The girls rushed to the Secret Spy Society as quickly as their legs could carry them. They crashed through the living room and burst into chatter. The other spies gathered around to listen.

Virginia glanced at her watch. "This ceremony is happening . . . now?" The girls nodded.

"Time for action!" said Nancy Wake with a tricky grin.

Miss Khan nodded solemnly. "We usually prefer to be discreet, but time is of the essence."

Josephine whirled into her jacket as she called for Chiquita. "I love a black-tie affair!"

Peggy, Rita, and Dot looked at one another in horror as they realized they were still wearing Virginia's old scouting uniforms.

"But what will we wear?" cried Peggy.

Josephine grinned. "I think we have some friends who can help!"

"You need *our* help?" Yuki and Cece looked completely baffled. The Fashion Twins stood in the entranceway of their store while snow powdered Peggy, Rita, Dot, and the Lady Spies. Peggy shrugged, equally surprised at the turn of events. It's not often that a spy asks the clientele for help.

Cece blinked. "Please, come in!" The Fashion Twins led them into the studio.

"So, what exactly do you need?" asked Yuki, settling down with a notebook in her lap.

Rita explained the situation.

Their eyes lit up. "You mean you want outfits?" Cece cried.

The girls nodded, and the Fashion Twins flew into action.

Cece pulled out a measuring tape. "We love children's wear!"

"So petite! So cute!" said Yuki, furiously sketching.

They zipped around the studio in a blur. Yarns whipped off of spools, needles were threaded deftly, pieces of fabric floated in the air, and buttons rolled across the floor.

Through a cloud of snipping, stitching, zigging, and zagging, three outfits appeared. "Give them a go!" Cece and Yuki cheered in unison.

The girls stepped into the small fitting rooms in the front of the shop and wiggled into their new outfits.

"*Hooray!*" cheered Cece.

"*Stunning!*" said Yuki. The Fashion Twins high-fived and the Lady Spies applauded.

The girls turned to look at one another and shrieked. "We look like the Lady Spies!" said Peggy. They grinned, feeling sparkly and special.

Dot turned to the Fashion Twins. "Thank you!" she said.

The Fashion Twins smiled, perfectly in sync. "Let's just call this an exchange for *your* help!"

— ✳ — ✳ — ✳ —

At seven o'clock, the girls and the Lady Spies gathered at the address on the invitation, which turned out to be a huge ballroom in the center of town. Outside, crowds of beautifully dressed and fantastically tuxedoed people mingled about and slowly drifted inside.

"Wow," said Peggy, starstruck. Rita gazed around with big eyes and Dot fidgeted with her hat.

Virginia gave them a smile. "You girls fit right in," she said softly. "Confidence is key when going undercover." The girls stood a little taller, determined not to let the knots in their stomachs get the best of them.

The girls drifted into the lobby, where their thoughts were interrupted by a *=Psssst!=* from the plants. Eyes peered back at them. The scouts! Dot pretended to tie her shoe while Rita and Peggy acted casual.

"What now?" hissed Finch.

"Just wait for the sign!" whispered Rita. "Chiquita is going to stay with you!"

Finch looked confused. "Who's Chiqui—" Suddenly the cheetah was at his side and gave him a headbutt on his arm.

"Don't worry, she's friendly!" said Dot, giving Chiquita a pat to demonstrate. "See?"

Finch eyed the cheetah nervously. "Doing Scout Leader's laundry for the rest of my life might be better than this."

Just then, a doorman called from the entrance. "Opening remarks are starting soon!"

"We gotta go!" hissed Dot, poking the others.

"But what about the sign?!" asked Finch.

"You'll know it when it happens!" called Peggy as they hurried through the front doors.

inside, the girls floated through crowds of towering adults and found their way to a good spot, conveniently next to the hors d'oeuvres. The girls peeked casually to their left and right, where the Lady Spies had dissolved into the crowd. Virginia winked as the lights dimmed and a tuxedoed man stepped onto the stage.

"Good evening, esteemed guests!" he spoke into the microphone with a charismatic grin. "We gather tonight to celebrate Scout Leader Smith's selfless

contributions to the children of the community"
—Peggy, Rita, and Dot rolled their eyes—"and
to commemorate her service with this prestigious
award!" The crowd erupted into applause as Scout
Leader walked onstage. Rita elbowed Peggy and Dot.
"Her dress!" she whispered. Onstage, Scout Leader
was draped in a twinkling gown. "That's the one she
stole!" hissed Peggy.

Scout Leader made her way to the microphone and accepted a trophy and envelope. "Thank you, thank you!" she said in a voice that made the girls feel itchy. "When I met my current scouts, they were undisciplined and lazy"—the girls stifled a laugh—"but I have single-handedly transformed them into efficient, conscientious citizens."

The crowd applauded again.

"What a hero!" said a woman.

"So generous!" said a man, wiping a single tear from his cheek.

Scout Leader cleared her throat. "Well, I must return to leading the scouts!" She stepped away from the microphone.

Dot nudged Peggy. "It's now or never!" she whispered.

With her hands shaking, Peggy nodded and raised two fingers to her lips. "Three . . . two . . . one . . ."

fwoooot!

she whistled.

At first, nothing seemed to happen. Peggy let out a nervous chuckle.

But then came the sound of galloping feet.

Eeeeeek!

shrieked Scout Leader.

Chiquita leaped across the ballroom and stood fiercely, blocking the exit door.

"Stop right there!" The scouts burst through the side door.

Scout Leader looked astonished. "Oh, hello, children," she said nervously.

The children closed in. "Care to explain this?" Finch pulled out the photograph of Scout Leader camping, while Doc held up the *Scout Leader Handbook*. "We quit!" the scouts shouted in unison. "This woman is a fraud!" Finch cried. "She's no scout leader."

Scout Leader turned
to run away but instead
found herself face-to-face
with the Petite Private Eyes. "And
it's time to return that dress you
stole!" Peggy said.

Scout Leader Smith began to sob
dramatically. "I've been caught!"

Though their feet hurt from their fancy shoes and all they wanted was a cup of cocoa, the Petite Private Eyes trudged back through town with the scouts, the Lady Spies, and the cheetah in tow. They were headed to the Fashion Twins' shop to share the good news: their dress had been found and Scout Leader Smith was banned from scouting for life!

"I'm happy we don't have to do those terrible scout duties anymore. But now we don't have a scout leader!" cried Darling, wiping a tear from her cheek.

"I still want to be a *real* scout," Doc said.

They opened the door of the shop, where they were greeted kindly by Yuki and Cece.

Rita started to explain the day's events to the Fashion Twins and pointed at the crestfallen troop of scouts when suddenly Finch interrupted excitedly, "Is that . . . a sewing machine?" The other scouts gasped as they caught a glimpse of the Fashion Twins' workspace. "Look at all the needles and thread!"

"Our Sewing and Textiles Badge!" cried Toots.

Doc's eyes lit up. "We never *did* get to learn how to sew!" she said, breathless with excitement.

The Fashion Twins exchanged looks.

Rita had a brilliant idea! She turned to Yuki and Cece. "Have you ever thought about being twin Scout Leaders?"

"Well, I do love camping," Cece said.

"And I think this troop needs some new uniforms," Yuki replied.

"Absolutely!" the Fashion Twins both agreed.

The scouts cheered, the Petite Private Eyes hugged Cece and Yuki, and the Lady Spies watched proudly as Chiquita gave an approving snort.

That night in Rita's attic, the girls toasted their cocoa (with extra marshmallows) over a job well done. A group of scouts had found a new home, a dress was rescued, and the Petite Private Eyes (and one cheetah) got some well-earned rest.

Virginia Hall (affectionately called Dindy by her family) grew up in Baltimore, Maryland, where she spent lots of time outside hunting and exploring. Rather than getting married and starting a family like her mother wanted, Virginia rejected convention and chose to travel across Europe. After witnessing the growth of Nazi control in Austria, she got involved in the resistance efforts. Tragedy struck during a hunting outing when Virginia accidentally shot herself in the foot, leading to the amputation of her left leg from the knee down. Virginia was devastated by the fateful turn of events, and pain would haunt her for the rest of her life. But with the aid of her prosthetic leg (a clunky, heavy contraption she nicknamed Cuthbert), Virginia was soon recruited to join the Special Operations Executive as a secret agent.

Many people at the time, including the Nazis, believed that women were docile and incapable of unconventional activities like espionage. Therefore, no one suspected a thing when Virginia began her first undercover assignment posing as a journalist.

She wrote stories for the *New York Post* that secretly contained clues for American and British officers. Soon Virginia's notoriety grew, earning her the infamous name "the Limping Lady," as she was hotly pursued by German Secret Police.

Virginia was a natural leader and formed a group of ragtag resistance operators, charming everyone from hairdressers and hoteliers to farmers and railway workers. Virginia's apartment was buzzing with resistance fighters, and her large network was instrumental in the storming of Normandy in 1944.

After the war, Virginia began working at what would later become the CIA. While she had no children of her own, Virginia doted lovingly on her many nieces and had a total of *five* French poodles.

ABOUT UNDERCOVER OPERATIONS

Throughout her time as a spy, Virginia was involved in many undercover operations. Because Cuthbert gave her a unique walk, some people overlooked or underestimated her, which became an excellent asset for missions (and better yet, she could even hide secret messages in her hollow wooden heel!).

On one of her more elaborate undercover operations, Virginia was placed in the French countryside and disguised as an elderly milkmaid. While selling her milk and cheese, she was able to listen to private conversations and distribute secret information. In order to do so, she had to dramatically change her appearance. She dyed her hair gray, learned to paint her face, and even had her teeth ground down to change her smile. Her disguise had to be perfect, right down to the buttons: she had to be sure that they were sewn the French way (parallel) rather than the American or British way (crisscross). Even the smallest detail could give away her covert mission.

But secret disguises don't always need to be so complex. When trying to hide her identity, Virginia often put on a wide hat or changed her hairstyle. Other times, she made her laugh very distinct or changed the way she walked by slipping things into her shoe. Sometimes she even stuffed bits of cloth or food into her cheeks to puff them out and affect the way she talked. All of these changes were easy to make on the go, allowing Virginia to be several different people in a matter of hours.

These simple tactics are perfect for spies in training. Try wearing a funny hat that draws attention away from your face or change the way you walk by borrowing a pair of shoes that are too big. Or, just like for Peggy, Rita, and Dot, wearing a trusty pair of cool sunglasses can always do the trick.

ABOUT THE OTHER LADY SPIES

SARAH AARONSOHN (1890-1917)
Syria. Founded and led an underground network of Jewish spies during World War I.

JOSEPHINE BAKER (1906-1975)
United States. Baker worked as a successful dancer, singer, and actress in France, where she was recruited to aid the French Resistance during World War II. A civil rights activist and entertainment icon, she also had a pet cheetah named Chiquita.

YOLANDE BEEKMAN (1911–1944)

Great Britain. Spoke several languages, which made her especially useful for secretive communications for the Special Operations Executive during World War II.

MARY JANE RICHARDS DENMAN (C. 1840–UNKNOWN)

United States. Also known as Mary Bowser, Denman was a formerly enslaved woman who went undercover in the Confederate South to fight against slavery as a Union Army spy.

SARAH EMMA EDMONDS (1841–1898)

Canada. Disguised herself as a man to help fight against slavery in the Civil War and work as a spy for the Union Army.

CHRISTINE GRANVILLE (1908-1952)

Poland. Also known as Krystyna Skarbek, she was known for her glamour, her style, and her ability to charm everyone (even guard dogs) as she worked for the Special Operations Executive during World War II.

ODETTE HALLOWES (1912-1995)

Great Britain. Proved herself invaluable to her team at the Special Operations Executive despite her nervous demeanor. Also a mother of three girls, she survived the Ravensbrück concentration camp.

NOOR INAYAT KHAN (1914-1944)

Great Britain. An author of stories and poems for young children, Khan worked as a wireless operator for the Special Operations Executive during World War II. Tragically, she was captured and sent to the Dachau concentration camp. She refused to give up any secrets to her captors, and her final word was rumored to be "liberty."

CECILY LEFORT (1900–1945)

Great Britain. Served in the Women's Auxiliary Air Force and for the Special Operations Executive during World War II. She had excellent manners and liked sailing boats and riding horses.

VIOLETTE SZABO (1921–1945)

France. Worked for the Special Operations Executive during World War II and was highly trained in many specialties, like navigation, demolition, and parachuting. (She could also tell very good jokes.)

NANCY WAKE (1912–2011)

New Zealand. Celebrated for her skills in combat and infamous for her sassy wit, she joined the French Resistance and the Special Operations Executive in World War II.